Little Bear & Brutus

BY ROBIN T. HARRISON

ILLUSTRATIONS BY GARY RAINSBARGER

Written by: Robin T. Harrison
Illustrations by: Gary Rainsbarger
Designed by: Susan Newman-Harrison
Proofed by: Vicky L Flanagan
Photo (page 30) by Susan Newman-Harrison
Photo and composition (page 27, 29) by: Dee Hunter

Library of Congress Control Number: Pending

ISBN 978-1-7337293-4-5

BY ROBIN T. HARRISON

TABLE OF CONTENTS

Prologue

Hi, I'm Rob. One night, I had a dream—a fuzzy dog appeared to me and said "Rob, I want you to record the conversations between Little Bear and Brutus." Of course I couldn't understand what he was talking about. I replied (remember, this is in a dream) "But dogs can't talk!" He replied "Oh yes they can. And, I'm going to arrange for you to understand Dog, so you can eavesdrop on these two little lovers." Well, I woke up and promptly forgot the dream. But then, I heard Little Bear and Brutus chatting... so, I wrote down what I heard them say to each other. Here it is.

Introduction

This little book is a transcription of conversations between two dog neighbors in Lake Arrowhead, California, a beautiful resort community high in the mountains, about 50 miles east of Los Angeles. There are many, many things to love about Lake Arrowhead, but the best thing is that most everybody who lives here has at least one dog. One of the dogs in this story, Brutus, has lived here for quite a long time. He is a medium/small Scottish Terrier look-alike. The other, Little Bear, is a Bichon Frise. Or, at least that is what her Mom and Dad say. A bit more about their stories and families follows. The two met for the first time shortly after Little Bear came home from the shelter.

New Friends Meet

Brutus: Woof! Woof. Wooof.

Little Bear: Woof? Woof?! Woof.

B: Good morning! You are new here, right?

L: Yes, I just arrived here at what I hope will be my forever home last night. It was a long ride in the car.

B: Well, welcome to the neighborhood! You will like it here, I'm sure. Your new Mom and Dad are friends of my Mom and Dad, and they say that they are very nice. My name is Brutus. Dad says I am named after a human person that was in a movie thousands of years ago, or something like that.

L: I am Little Bear. I come from a shelter somewhere in the desert. I don't really remember too much about what I did before I was at the shelter. While I was at the shelter, I had a roommate, a big dog named Gretel. She was nice. But, the day before Mom brought me here, she went with a young couple of human people who had a big place for her to play. They seemed genuinely lovely. I was happy for Gretel, but I was very lonely. But, the next day, this lady I call Mom took me away, too! I will miss the human people at the shelter who took care of me, but I am glad to be here.

B: (to himself—I am glad she is here, too. She is quite pretty.)

L: (to herself—He is a handsome fellow—I wonder if he has a girlfriend already?)

B: Let me tell you about my family. I have my Mom and my Dad and two other human people. I used to have my Dad's Dad and Mom. He was a great friend. But, they moved to the desert so he could play gof (golf in human), or something like that, every day. I've been to the desert, it is hot and dusty, and I don't like it. Bella lives here too, she is another dog person. We get along pretty well, but, she is quiet and just sleeps a lot of the time.

L: Oh, that is interesting. I have my Mom, who brought me here, and my Dad, who says I am his dog. I also have another person called Petey. He is a cat. He isn't real nice to me, I don't know why. I didn't try to take his food or anything.

B: Yes, I have met your cat. We didn't get along too well, either.

L: I hear my Dad calling me. I'd love to chat some more. Is it OK if I come visit you? Will your Mom or Dad care?

B: Oh no, they will welcome you to come over. Come over any time, Little Bear.

L: Thank you. I'll see you later.

B: Bye!

Brutus Is Sick

Little Bear: Woof! Woof? Wooff.

Brutus: woof wooofff gruff.

L: Brutus, what is the matter? I've come to visit, and you wouldn't come out.

B: Little Bear, I have been so sick! I couldn't walk, I had to be carried out to poop, I was so sad.

L: Oh, Brutus, I am so sorry! Are you better now?

B: Yes, a little better.

L: My Dad says your Dad is the best doctor anywhere. He will make you healthy again, I'm sure.

B: But he is a human person doctor, not a dog person doctor.

L: Doesn't matter. Human people and dog people are a lot the same. Besides, you are better, aren't you?

B: Yes, some. But Little Bear, I am so scared of dying.

L: You are not going to die, Brutus. I would miss you too much. You are my boyfriend, you know.

B: I hope you are right.

L: My Dad says "all dogs go to heaven." I don't really know what that means, Brutus. I guess it is kinda like a nice Bark Park, with lots of lovely green grass to go potty on, and where there are no mean big dogs, and no human person ever hurts a dog, and you can chase cars and bicycles whenever you want, and your humans give you bacon. Or something like that. Dad says that any human person that ever hurts a dog is not allowed in there, ever.

B: Well, I've heard of that place, but I don't want to go there just yet. I would miss you too much.

L: Don't worry, Boyfriend, everybody at my house, even Petey the mean old cat, is praying for you. My Dad says that is the best thing we can do. So we all are doing it!

B: Well Little Bear, having such a good friend like you makes me try hard to get better. But I'd better go in now; Dad says I need to rest. Thank you so much for coming over, and thank you for being my girlfriend. I love you lots!

L: Brutus, I love you too. See you soon.

Little Bear

114B

Little Bear Goes Flying

Brutus: Woof! Woof! WoofWoof!

Little Bear: Woof! Woof!

B: Where U been, Little Bear? I saw you leave with the big people this morning.

L: Well, Brutus, I went flying with Mom and Dad. They're pilots, you know.

B: What do you mean flying? What's a pilot?

L: In their airplane! Like a bird! Except it is really noisy.

B: What's an airplane?

L: Like a car, but it rises up like a bird, and flys to wherever the big people who are pilots want to go. We went to Snet Mer (Santa Maria in human language), or something like that. Dad had a long, long, boring talk with a man in a blue shirt. Dad said this man was his boss. But, I know Mom is his boss. Human people are very confused!

B: You are making this up! There is no such thing as an airplane!

L: No, Brutus, there is, really. Ask your Dad. He'll tell you. And my Dad has five of them. Well, they are really Mom's, but she lets Dad use them. I have seen Dad fly at something called an airshow, or something. He flys upside down tumbles like the crows!

B: I don't believe any of this! Besides, my Dad would never go in something like that.

L: Brutus, you should get my Dad to take you flying. You like to ride in the car; you can look out and see all the other animals, and smell all the trees, and like that. In an airplane, it's even better, 'cause you can see so much more.

B: No way! I'd never go in one of those things, even if they really do exist. Which I doubt.

L: OK, Brutus. You stay on the ground, like a worm or a snake. I'll go fly whenever I can. OOPS, C U later. Mom is yelling at me.

B: Little Bear, I don't believe you, one bit, but thanks for coming over anyhow. I'll see you soon.

L: Bye, Boyfriend! I love you.

Little Bear Goes To The Beach

Little Bear: Woof Woof Rrrf Woof!

Brutus: Woof Woooof!

L: Brutus, come out! I want to tell you about a field trip with my Mom and Dad!

B: I'm all ears, L.B. But even all ears, my ears aren't as big as yours.

L: Thank you. The groomer lady spends a lot of time on my ears, but that's not what I want to tell you about.

B: So what new adventure this time?

L: Mom and Dad and I went on a long drive in the truck. On the way to wherever we went, I mostly snoozed. Dad took some stuff to a guy he knows, I guess. The guy gave him an envelope with a lot of money in it. Dad smiled and told him "Thanks". I don't know what that was all about. But, on the way home, we stopped for lunch and Dad took me for a long walk.

B: That sounds nice. Where did you guys stop?

L: That is what I wanted to tell you! Dad called it a beach. It was fun to walk on. The ground was all soft, and there was a HUGE lake by the beach. Just like our lake here, except it was so big you couldn't see the other side!

B: I think that is called the ocean. I've been with my family a couple times. It is indeed huge.

L: I tried to drink some of the water, but it tasted awful. And Dad yelled at me.

B: That water would make you very sick! Your Dad was right!

L: Well I had a great time anyhow. The water in the lake sloshed back and forth, and I ran toward and away from the water, I didn't want to get wet. But, there were a couple of big dogs who were running around in the water. They said they were having a great time. But the water was cold, so I stayed out.

B: That's good, L.B. I went in the ocean once and the sloshing water almost carried me away! My Dad had to come in after me. And when I finally dried off, my fur was all stiff. I didn't like that much.

L: The other thing that happened was lots of Human people told Dad how cute I was. So of course, I had to prance around and be cute. That's my job assignment, you know.

B: You are so conceited, L.B.

L: Well, you have told me that you think I'm cute, too!

B: Yes, you are. I love you, and not just because you are cute.

L: Brutus, you are the nicest boyfriend in the whole world, I love you too. But, Mom is calling me. Gotta go, see you soon!

B: OK good-bye!

Brutus Says Little Bear Is Just Right

Little Bear: Woof Woof Wooff.

Brutus: Grf woof WOOF!

L: Hi Boyfriend! How are you feeling?

B: Better, Little Bear, better. My legs still hurt but I can walk a bit better. I can go down the ramp, but Mom or Dad has to help me back up. But I'm getting better.

L: Oh Brutus, that is such good news. I'm sure you will be OK very shortly. But, I came to chat about my Dad.

B: So what's new with your Dad?

L: He didn't think I could understand, but he called me fat! I am so hurt! Do you think I'm fat, Brutus?

B: Oh no, Bear! You are just right. You are beautiful!

L: I don't want to be fat Brutus. Dad said I gained 4 pounds. Do you know what a pound is? I don't.

B: Not really. I know all the big human people are all worried about pounds, though. Pounds must be really bad.

L: Dad said my gaining 4 pounds was like him gaining 80 pounds. Does that make any sense to you, Brutus?

B: Not any sense at all. Sometimes I think human people aren't very smart.

L: Well if you don't think I'm fat, that is what matters to me.

B: No, you are just right.

L: I gotta go. Dad is going to the hangar, where he works on his airplane. I get to sleep on a nice comfy bed while he works away. Sometimes he hurts himself, and asks me to lick to help heal up his ouchy. I don't like it when he hurts himself.

B: Now you are trying to convince me there are such things as airplanes. I still don't believe that.

L: Oh yes there are. Dad has shown your Mom and Dad pictures. Ask to see them. Gotta go, Dad is yelling! Love you Brutus!

B: Thanks for coming over—See you soon. Love you too!

A Huge Bear

Little Bear: WOOF WOOF WOOF WOOF-WOOF!

Brutus: Little Bear! What is It?

L: Brutus, come out I gotta talk to you!

B: OK, OK. Here I am. What is the commotion?

L: Brutus, when I went out for my evening walk last night with my Dad, I saw this huge dog! He or she was brown and very shaggy. He was really fat! Not like my Dad called me. Dad called me urgently, told me to run inside right away. He ran in too! Why would he do that?

B: Little Bear, that wasn't a dog person. That was a bear person! They are very ferocious, and they eat dogs like us.

L: What? WHAT?? I've never heard of such a thing. I am a bear. That is my name. Why would a bear person eat me?

B: You are named Bear. Your Dad is also named Bear. But you are not a bear, you are a dog. Your Dad is not a bear, he is a human. Bear persons are very different. They speak a different language, they live in the forest, and they come out at night to the human person places, to raid the garbage cans. One tore the door right off of Mom's garbage hut. She was very upset by that. Bear persons are really

mean. They will eat anybody!

L: Oh Brutus, that is very sad. If this bear person comes again, I will try to be his/her friend. Then he won't eat me.

B: Little Bear, listen to me. Mr., or Ms., as the case may be, Bear does not want to be your friend. He/she wants to eat you! Please, please listen to your Dad. He was smart to get you inside the house as quickly as possible. Bears are not nice.

L: But everybody says cats aren't nice either, and I have a cat that lives with me, and he doesn't try to eat me.

B: Little Bear, you are being naïve. Cats are little. He would eat you if he could, but he knows your Mom and Dad would whap him if he tried to eat you. Cats are mean, but they are also smart. Your cat isn't going to try to eat you. The bear would if he/she had a chance. Please, Little Bear, I love you too much for you to get eaten.

L: OK, Brutus, thank you for the lesson. I will avoid the bear. How are you doing?

B: Much better, thank you. But, I have to go back to sleep, Dad wants me to rest.

L: OK. Love you. Have a good rest.

Little Bear Was In A Car Crash

Brutus: Woof Woof rff Woof!

Little Bear: Woof Woof WOOF!

B: Little Bear, where you been? I haven't seen you for a while.

L: Oh Brutus, terrible news! I was in a car crash!

B: Oh no! Are you OK?

L: Yes, I think so. When it happened, I was thrown around like a frisbee. I crashed into the dashboard—that's the part of the car in front of where my Mom and Dad sit. I heard them call it that.

B: That's terrible! Are your Mom and Dad OK?

L: Yes, I think so. Dad was outside the car. Mom was in her chair, and got pushed all around! The car was parked, and some guy just drove his truck into it at about 100 miles per hour! As fast as you can run! It made a terrible loud noise.

B: Is the car OK?

L: No. I heard Dad crying. He loves that car, and he says maybe it can't be fixed. But, he took it to a friend of his, who said he would fix it. But, it will cost a lot of money, I heard Mom say. I don't know much about money, Brutus. What did Mom mean?

B: I don't know too much about money either, Little Bear. My Mom and Dad don't talk about it much. But, what I think is that it is like favors— if you have money, you can get stuff you want.

L: You mean like dog treats?

B: Well, dogs don't have money. We pretty much have to be nice to human people to get what we want. But, human people can get dog food and treats and fancy costumes for us if they have money and give it to the people that have the stuff we need.

L: So can Dad's car get fixed if he gives his friend money? I hope so, because I love to ride in that car. It is very comfy. I have a whole back seat just for me.

B: I really don't know, Little Bear. I guess it depends on how much money your Dad gives his friend.

L: This money stuff confuses me, Brutus. I like our system of favors better. I wonder why human people can't do that?

B: That's a great mystery, I agree. But, they can't seem to ever agree on how many favors a human needs to do to get his car fixed, I guess. So that's why they use money. It's just paper, not even big enough to use on the ground. Human people are very strange!

L: Well, maybe so, but my Mom and Dad are very good to me. Look at me, Brutus. I just got back from the Groomer Lady!

B: You are the most beautiful lady dog I have ever seen. That is one reason why I love you so much.

L: Oh Brutus, you are the best boyfriend ever. I love you too!

New Dog Friends

Little Bear: Woof Woooof!

Brutus: Woof Woof Woof?

L: Morning Boyfriend! How are you today?

B: Pretty good, Little Bear. My back still hurts a bit. I'm old, you know.

L: Brutus, you are not old. You are a fine dog. My Dad says you are a fine dog. And I know you are. But, Dad says his back hurts a bit sometimes too. He says he is old. I hope not. I don't know much about being old.

B: I don't either. But my Mom says I am old. Humans say all kinds of dumb stuff.

L: Yes they do. Anyhow, I went on a field trip with Mom and Dad yesterday. They wanted to have lunch at a Chinese Restaurant in Rnng-spgs (Running Springs in human). Or somewhere like that. So we all three went there in the Jeep. I met a HUGE dog there! He was very nice. He was as big as the big dogs I see human people riding on! And there was another dog there, too.

B: Those big dogs that humans ride aren't really dogs, my Dad calls them horses. I tried to talk to one of them once, but he couldn't understand me. But, tell me about the dogs you met.

L: Well like I said, one was VERY big. He was white, with nice black spots. He told me he was very happy to meet me. He was quire handsome, but not as handsome as you are, Boyfriend. The other dog was about the same size as me, and she was also very nice. She was wearing a pink, frilly dress. It looked quite stylish. Her Mom told Mom and Dad that she was French. I'm not sure what that means. Do you know, Brutus?

B: I think that means she was from France. France is a place far, far away, where dogs and their human people live, and they talk funny.

L: Well, that explains why I couldn't understand a word of what she said. She kept saying "wee, wee". Dunno what that means.

B: I suppose that is what French humans and dogs say when they mean "yes". But I'm not sure.

L: Brutus, you are so smart. How did you learn all of these things?

B: Sometimes I pretend to be sleeping when Mom and Dad talk about stuff. But, I try to pay attention.

L: Yeah, I do that. But, my Mom and Dad usually talk about airplanes. Not about France.

B: There you go again Little Bear, trying to convince me there is such a thing as an airplane.

L: Brutus, all you have to do is look up when you hear a hissing kinda roar and you will see one of them.

B: Ok, ok, but I still don't believe you. Gotta go, Mom just put my dinner in my special plate. Love you, Little Bear!

L: Love you too, Brutus. Have a good dinner!

A Visiting Dog

Little Bear: Woof Woof WOOF! W O O F !!

Brutus: woof woof woof

L: Brutus! You awake?

B: I am now (yawn).

L: Brutus, we need to talk. There was another dog up here last night. He is bigger than either of us, and black and white all over. What do you think about that?

B: Oh yeah. That is Jones. He lives down on Banff. His human people let him out at night, and he travels all over the place.

L: Oh my goodness. Isn't that dangerous for him?

B: I guess it is. I'm happy to have my nice kennel here, where it is cool in the summer and warm in the winter and I have my two human people to bring me food and give me baths and comb my hair so everybody says I'm very handsome.

L: Well you are indeed very handsome. I'm proud to have you for my boyfriend. But tell me about Jones. He is black and white all over?

B: Yep. Funny thing about that—none of the dog people are surprised that he is black and white, but human people always make some comment about his color. I don't know why.

L: Yes, I've heard comments from some human people. They seem to make a big deal about other human's color. Do you know why they do?

B: No, I don't understand it either. What does it matter what color a person is? Well, like I said, human people aren't very smart. But, we have to put up with them, 'cause they give us food. I guess. I'd hate to have to get my own food, like my cousin Timber Wolf has to. He says that he wishes somebody would give him food so he could relax, like I do all day. We are lucky, Little Bear.

L: Yes, Brutus, we are. My Mom and Dad love me more than anything. I love you more than anything. You are the best boyfriend. When I was at the shelter, before Mom and Dad adopted me, I had a big dog person friend who was tan and black. The human people who adopted her didn't seem to care about her color. What color is Timber?

B: Gray. Maybe now silver, he's getting pretty old. Nobody, dog or human, cares about his color. So I don't understand the human people. Like I said, not too smart.

L: Yes, Brutus, too bad they aren't as smart as dogs. Well, I better go, time for me to have dinner.

B: Goodbye, Sweetheart. Have a nice dinner.

L: Bye, Brutus. See you soon.

Little Bear Goes To Arizona

Brutus: Woof! Woof! Wooof!

Little Bear: Woof! Rff!

B: Little Bear, where you been? I haven't seen you for a while!

L: Well, Brutus, I went on a long field trip with my Mom and Dad. We went to Zonia, (Arizona to human people) or some place like that. And we stayed in a place where human people called Indoans, or something like that, stayed a long time ago. It was really fun! I got to walk all over lots of old places, up and down. I was tired by evening every day.

B: Bear, I think they are called Indians, not Indoans. They were human people that lived here before a different kind of human people came here. Human people like our Moms and Dads. They came from a place called Europe, a long ways away.

L: We met some Indian ladies, they were very nice. They said they had a dog person like me, but the dog was not with them but was at home with the kids. That makes me sad, Brutus, dogs should always be with their Mom and Dad. What are kids?

B: Kids are young, small human people. Sometimes when the Mom and Dad have to go work the dog stays home and watches the small human people, to make sure they don't get into trouble. I used to watch my Mom and Dad's little humans, but they were always getting into some trouble! They are all big and grownup now.

L: Hm, that's interesting. I wondered why some humans are little, and some are big. Like puppies, I guess. But anyhow, let me tell you about the field trip.

B: Yes, please do. I'd like to hear.

L: We drove and drove and drove. It took all day to get to Zonia. When we got there, Mom went into a building, and came back with keys to get into our new little house, and a whole bunch of papers. Mom and Dad looked at the papers, and said "Let's do that"—"Let's do this"—"Yes, that will be fun". So the first thing we did was go on a dirt road for miles and miles, through a forest. It was kind of a strange forest, not all green and cool like our forest here, but dusty and dry. Then we went to a place where the old Indians lived, long ago. It was not in very good shape, but Mom and Dad said it was a wonderful place.

Then we went to a big house that had all kinds of stuff I didn't understand, but Dad thought it was great. It had machines, and shiny metal stuff. I was bored, but the guys there said they wanted a picture of me, so that was good. Then we went to some more Indian places, one way up on a mountain. And I got to walk all around, and of course everybody who saw me said how cute I was. And after dinner each night, I got to sleep with Mom and Dad in their big bed. I liked that. Then we drove and drove and drove and got home. Except Mom made Dad stop several times so she could buy stuff from the Indian ladies.

B: All that sounds exciting. Little Bear. You are lucky you get to travel so much. I appreciate your sharing these adventures with me.

L: Brutus, you are so nice to listen to my stories. You are the best boyfriend anywhere!

B: Woops! I hear your mom calling. See you later Girlfriend! Love ya!

L: Love you too, B!

Little Bear Looks So Pretty

Brutus: Woof Woof Woof!!

Little Bear: Woof! Rf! Woorf!

B: Little Bear, I saw you leave with the big Human People this morning. Where did you go?

L: Mom went shopping, Dad stayed in the car, and I went to the groomer lady. Can't you tell?

B: Yes indeed. You look even more lovely than usual. Is that a new ear-do?

L: I think so, I heard Mom and Pam, the groomer lady, talk about it. You like it?

B: Oh yes. Very becoming.

L: (Coyly) There was a very handsome German fellow there who said it was pretty, too.

B: Little Bear, are you trying to make me jealous? I thought I was your boyfriend.

L: Well, a girl likes to hear she looks nice. But yes, Brutus, you are my boyfriend and my only boyfriend. I'm sorry if I hurt your feelings.

B: No, I understand. Of course I am jealous, you are the prettiest lady dog I have ever seen.

L: Brutus, you are so nice. I don't need any boyfriend but you! You might see if you can get your mom to take you to see Pam. Lots of boy dogs go there, to get ready for big dog shows. You are very handsome and would be even more handsome if Pam groomed you. I'll bet you could win dog shows!

B: Oh, thanks, but I don't think so. Remember I have a cousin who is a wolf. Those snooty dog show dogs wouldn't even talk to me.

L: Well, I think a wolf cousin is the best thing a dog can have! I want to meet Timber some time. But, I don't care about those show dogs, anyhow. They are very stuck-up, I agree. There was a snooty Pomeranian at Pam's getting ready for a show, and all she would talk about is herself. What a bore.

B: Little Bear, you are a terrific girlfriend. I am so lucky to have you.

L: Likewise, Boyfriend. But, here comes Dad and I have to make a production out of saying hello. C U later! Love you!

B: Samo samo L.B. Bye!

Little Bear In The Snow

Brutus: Woof. Woof. WOOOF!

Little Bear: Woof! Wrf. Wrf.

B: Little Bear! Where have you been? I haven't seen you for a long while.

L: I've been stuck in this white stuff! I heard Mom call it snow, or something. Mom shoveled some of it out of the way, so I could go potty. Dad shoveled a path so I could come over.

B: Yes it is called snow. And it has covered the ground in my dog run, but it is very cold, so I stayed inside. But you always bark for me to come out, and I didn't hear you bark for the longest time. I was worried about you.

L: That is so sweet of you, Brutus. I've missed you too. But, tell me about this snow stuff—where does it come from? Does it fall down out of the sky like rain? Why does it stay around? The rain just runs away, before I can drink it or anything.

B: Yes, it falls from the sky. It is really rain that is frozen from the cold. When the sun comes out, it will go away. But it takes a while.

L: Well, I hope it goes away. When I go out, it makes my tummy cold! And I can't smell around for other dogs or animals. I don't know who has been here! Dad says he saw some footprints from Jones, but I can't tell. Everything is under this snow stuff!

B: Don't worry, Little Bear. It always goes away. My dad said that a cold winter with lots of snow is good for us, because it will keep our lake full. Everybody likes that! When the lake is full, I get to go on the boat. Have you been on a boat, Little Bear?

L: Sure! I went with my Aunt Marcia and my Aunt Jill on their boats. I like going on boats, so I'm glad the lake will be filled up.

B: I heard my Dad say we were going to have some more snow, so make sure your Dad shovels a path so you can come to visit, OK?

L: I'll do that. I miss you when we can't talk. And I'll be glad when this snow stops, so we can both come out and play. But I better go now, I'm getting cold.

B: Me too! See you soon. Love you, Girlfriend!

L: Same, Boyfriend! Be safe and warm. I'll come as often as I can.

Little Bear Buys A New Car

Brutus: Woof! Woof! Woof!!

Little Bear: Worf. WOOF!

B: Little Bear, I saw your Dad in a spiffy new car. What is that all about?

L: Yes, I bought it for him as a surprise.

B: What?! Dogs don't have money. Cars cost lots of money. My Mom and Dad got a new car, and they said it cost lots of money. How could you buy it?

L: Well, I had my Mom help me. But, let me tell you the story. One night at dinner Dad showed Mom a picture of this car. He called it a Stinkway, I think. He said it was a great car, but there weren't any for sale, all of them that were ever made were taken.

B: Little Bear, please! It is a Stingray, not a Stinkway, named after a ferocious fish that can swim very fast. Those cars are magic! Like the fish. So how did you get it?

L: Well, that's the story. Mom called all over on the telephone, and finally found a guy that had one, just the right color, silver with black chairs. So she went to see it. It was in Sen Drago, or someplace like that, a long way from here.

B: That's San Diego, almost to Mexico, a long ways for sure. So then what happened?

L: Mom wrote on a piece of paper, and shook hands with this guy, and we came home. Then the next day, after Dad had gone to the airport

to work on the airplane again, we picked up Aunt Margi, and took her to the Jeep, and we all went to get the car. I rode home with Margi in the Jeep, 'cause Mom was worried about me scratching the new car. Then we took it to Dad at the airport. He nearly fainted! All his friends came to look at the new car. It made quite a stir.

B: Well I believe that! That is a great car. Have you gotten to ride in it yet?

L: Yes with Dad driving and Mom holding me. I like that because I can see out and bark at other dogs and enjoy the scenery. I rode on the seat without Mom once, but Dad went real fast, and it scared me. So he slowed down and I was fine.

B: That car is the fastest car in the world, Little Bear. Your Dad is really lucky you bought it for him. I know he loves it. And, he loves you.

L: Yes, Dad is lucky to have me. But, I am lucky to have him and Mom. And you, Boyfriend. How are things with you?

B: Better, Little Bear, better. I feel pretty good. And, I always feel better when you come for a visit. I miss you!

L: I miss you too! I do come as often as I can. I really like it when your Dad brings you out so we can play together. You are the best boyfriend a girl dog ever had.

B: Thank you Girlfriend. I love you a heap.

L: I love you too, Brutus. See you soon.

PHOTO BY DEE HUNTER

Epilogue

I hope you have enjoyed these conversations. I did my very best
to scribble down what these two friends said to each other. Some
of you may think I just made all of this up. Well, you have a right
to think that. But, I didn't. And if you listen carefully enough, I'll
bet you could learn to understand Dog, too. —Rob

About The Author

Robin T. Harrison

Rob and his wife Susan live in a house with a three hundred sixty degree view on top of a mountain in the resort community of Lake Arrowhead, fifty miles east of Los Angeles, California. Here they share space with Little Bear and Petey the cat.

Rob is an aeronautical engineer, a registered safety engineer, a retired lawyer, and a professional airshow stunt pilot. He enjoys maintaining and modifying his own aircraft. He spent thirty years with the U S Forest Service, starting as a fire fighter in Oregon and retiring as Program Leader for Aviation at the San Dimas Technology and Development Center in Southern California.